Kisa Kids Publications
4415 Fortran Court
San Jose, CA 95134
(260) KISA KID
(260) 547-2543
info@kisakids.org

Dedication

This book is dedicated to the beloved grandson of the Noble Prophet (ṣ), Imām Ḥusayn (ʿa), who, along with his loyal and brave companions, was martyred thirsty on the plains of Karbala, near the banks of a flowing river and were denied even a drop of water. The Prophet (ṣ) is quoted to have said, "Ḥusayn is from me and I am from Ḥusayn."

Acknowledgments

Prophet Muḥammad (ṣ): The pen of a writer is mightier than the blood of a martyr.

True reward lies with Allah, but we would like to sincerely thank Sisters Binte Zehra Naqvi, Nida Syed, Nazeera Salak, Abir Rashid, Sabika Mithani, Marwa Kachmar and Abeda Khimji for their efforts. May Allah bless them in this world and the next.

Transliteration

Arabic has been transliterated according to the following key:

ء	a, u, i (initial form)	ز	z	ك	k	◌َ	a
ء	ʾ	س	s	ل	l	◌ُ	u
ب	b	ش	sh	م	m	◌ِ	i
ت	t	ص	ṣ	ن	n	◌َا	ā
ث	th	ض	ḍ	ه	h	◌ُو	ū
ج	j	ط	ṭ	و	w (as a consonant)	◌ِي	ī
ح	ḥ	ظ	ẓ	ي	y (as a consonant)		
خ	kh	ع	ʿ	ة	ah (without iḍāfah)		
د	d	غ	gh	ة	at (with iḍāfah)		
ذ	dh	ف	f	ال	al-		
ر	r	ق	q				

Preface

Prophet Muḥammad (ṣ): Nurture and raise your children in the best way. Raise them with the love of the Prophets and the Ahl al-Bayt ('a).

وَجَعَلْنَا مِنَ الْمَاءِ كُلَّ شَيْءٍ حَيٍّ

"…and We have made everything out of water…" (21:30)

Children are born with a pure fiṭrah, mind and heart, and should be taught from childhood to appreciate the blessings of Allah, how to value them, how to properly use them and especially not waste them. One such blessing is water. Children should know the importance of water, the immense mercy of Allah for this bounty, and how valuable it is. For example, if children knew how many thousands of droplets make one glass of water or how would life be without this blessing, they would appreciate and value this blessing more.

Knowing this at a young age makes children responsible members of the community and contributing global citizens in being conscious to conserve water, take care of the environment and preserve nature.

Literature is an influential form of media that often shapes the thoughts and views of an entire generation. Therefore, in order to establish an Islamic foundation for future generations, there is a dire need for compelling Islamic literature. Over the past several years, this need has become increasingly prevalent throughout Islamic centers and schools everywhere. Due to the growing dissonance between parents, children, society, and the teachings of Islam and the Ahl al-Bayt ('a), this need has become even more pressing. Al-Kisa Foundation, along with its subsidiary, Kisa Kids Publications, was conceived in an effort to help bridge this gap with the guidance of 'ulamā' and the help of educators. We would like to make this a communal effort and platform. Therefore, we sincerely welcome constructive feedback and help in any capacity.

We pray to Allah to give us the strength and tawfīq to perform our duties and responsibilities.

With Du'as,
Nabi R. Mir (Abidi)

*Disclaimer: Religious texts have **not** been translated verbatim so as to meet the developmental and comprehension needs of children.*

Please recite a Sūrah al-Fātiḥah for:

Marḥūmīn of Kasim family
Marḥūm Syed Ali Kasim Abidi
Marḥūmah Sara Kasim

Marḥūmah Naeema Kazmi

Marḥūm Mohammad Raza Syed

RAHMAH THE RAINDROP

Written by: Binte Zehra Naqvi•Illustrated by: Nida Syed

Kisa Kids Publications

Under the Guidance of Moulana Nabi R. Mir (Abidi)

وَٱللَّهُ أَنزَلَ مِنَ ٱلسَّمَآءِ مَآءً فَأَحْيَا بِهِ ٱلْأَرْضَ بَعْدَ مَوْتِهَا

"And Allah has sent down water from the sky with which He revives the earth after its death…" [16:65]

Drip, drop, drippity drop.
Down came a raindrop.

Her name was Rahmah!
Rahmah, the raindrop.

Wheeeee!

exclaimed Rahmah, with her heart full of
joy as she was about to fall into the ocean.

Suddenly, the wind came WHOOSHING and SWOOSHING, taking her far, far away...

...far, far away onto the land where there was no sign of the ocean!

Just then, Rahmah heard a voice,
"Hello! Who is there?!"
Rahmah looked right and left
but did not see anyone.

"Hello, down here!"
Came the voice again.

Rahmah looked down.

There he was.
Down on the ground,
dry and withered,
a little seed was found.

"Salāmun ʿalaykum!* My name is Rahmah."
"Waʿalaykum salām, Rahmah. Can you please help me?" the seed pleaded.
"How can I help you?" asked Rahmah.

---

* ā is an elongated "a" sound, like "aa"; ʿa is from the middle of the throat

"Oh, you see, I am just a seed, but Allah created me to
be more than that. Allah created me to be a tree - a tree
full of fruit. However, you see, I have no water to grow.
Would you give me some water to grow?
Oh, please, pretty, pretty please!"

"Of course!" replied Rahmah, and she gave
the little seed some of her water.
The little seed drank the precious water
making sure not to waste even a tiny bit.

Over time, the little seed grew and grew,

first **stretching** his roots,

then **UP** rose his trunk

and then his branches
filled with fruit.

Rahmah was happy that she was able to help a creation of Allah. She wanted to stay and enjoy the yummy fruit, but she had to find her way back to the ocean.

So, she bid farewell and went on her way.

As Rahmah passed by the forest, she heard a cry.

Oh dear! I must find out what is wrong. Maybe I can help, thought Rahmah.

Deep down in the forest,
a plant let out a cry,
"My flowers used to bloom,
but now they are all dry."

"Is that why you are crying, my friend?" asked Rahmah.

Sniff, sob!

"Oh, you see, I am just a dried-up plant, but Allah created me to be more than that. Allah created me to be a rose bush full of roses. However, I have no water to grow. Would you give me some water to grow? Oh, please, pretty, pretty please!"

Hmmm... thought Rahmah. She had to find her way back to the ocean, but she also really wanted to help the rose bush. What should she do?

She decided to help the rose bush and share some of her water.
The rose bush drank the precious water making sure not to waste even a tiny bit.

Over time, the rose bush grew and grew.
Her roses **blossomed** and **bloomed**.
Their beautiful scent filled the air with a
most sweet and fragrant perfume.

Alḥamdulillāh![*] The plant thanked Allah for sending Rahmah to help her grow into a beautiful rose bush.

Rahmah was so happy that she was able to help a creation of Allah. She wanted to stay and smell the fragrant roses, but she had to find her way back to the ocean!

So, she bid farewell and went on her way, yet again.

*ḥ is a heavy "ha" sound from the middle of the throat; ā is an elongated "a" sound, like "aa"

Rahmah had not gotten too far when she
heard another sound. It was coming from a
bird who was lying down on the ground.

A little thirsty bird
lay breathless on the ground.
The scorching sun above
had left him flightless and earthbound.

"What is the matter, my friend?"
Rahmah asked the little bird.

"Oh, you see, I am just a little bird who is too tired to fly, but Allah created me to be more than that. Allah created me to be a bird that can soar. However, I have no water and I am oh-so-thirsty. Would you give me some water?
Oh, please, pretty, pretty please!"

Hmmm... thought Rahmah. She really, really wanted to help the little bird, but if she did, she would be too tired to get to the ocean. Even so, she did not want to say no to a creation of Allah, so she decided to help him and share some of her water.

The little bird drank the precious water making sure not to waste even a tiny bit.

The little bird, once so weak,
slowly found the strength to fly.
He flapped his wings and soared
up high into the sky.

Rahmah said goodbye to her friend as he flew up, up and away. She was happy that she was able to help a creation of Allah, but she was also sad that she hadn't yet reached the ocean. And after a long day of helping others, she was too tired to continue her journey.

Rahmah prayed to Allah, *Oh Allah, help me. Please help me get to the ocean!*

Just then, the little bird came back.

"Why are you sad Rahmah?" he asked.
Rahmah told the little bird everything, from how she was taken far, far away from the ocean, to how she was too tired to get back to it now.

"Hop on my back, and I will take you there!" the little bird said to Rahmah.

Rahmah got on his back. The little bird took Rahmah higher and higher until they found the ocean.

When Rahmah saw the ocean, she was so excited! She sincerely thanked the little bird and jumped off his back.

PLOP!

She fell into the water. At last, Rahmah was
united with the ocean.

All praise be to Allah
Who made me so,
to be more than just a raindrop.
He made me Rahmah, a mercy,
to the whole wide world.

The ocean gently surrounded and embraced
Rahmah. Being connected with the ocean
made Rahmah feel stronger and stronger.
She thanked Allah for all of His blessings.
Finally, she was home.

"...and We have made everything out of water..." (21:30)

The End.

Glossary

(ṣ): Peace and blessings be upon Prophet Muḥammad and his family

(swt): All Glory belongs to God, the Glorified and Exalted

(ʿa): Peace and blessings be upon him/her

Ahl al-Bayt: Divinely appointed family members of Prophet Muḥammad (ṣ)

Alḥamdulillāh: All praise is for God

al-Fātiḥah: The first chapter of the Qurʾān that is commonly recited and sent as a gift of prayer for the deceased

Allah: The Arabic term for God, a culmination of all His holy names and titles

Duʿā: Supplication; a confidential prayer between an individual and God

Imām: A divinely appointed leader, sometimes refers to a spiritual leader

InshāʾAllāh: God-willing

Marḥūmīn: Those who have passed away

Rahmah: Mercy; also the root word of the name of Allah ʿar-Raḥmān' (All Merciful)

Salāmun ʿalaykum: Peace be upon you

Tawfīq: Divine blessings from God that give one the opportunity and ability to thrive toward success

Wa ʿalaykum salām: And peace be upon you

ʿUlamāʾ: Scholars